An Elegy for Mathematics

An Elegy for Mathematics

small stories

Anne Valente

DURHAM, NORTH CAROLINA

AN ELEGY FOR MATHEMATICS

Library of Congress Cataloging-in-Publication Data

Valente, Anne
An Elegy for Mathematics: stories / by Anne Valente
p. cm.
ISBN-13: 978-0-9887044-0-4

Design and Production
Cover Art © 2013 by Nathan Pierce
Printed in the United States of America.

Published by
BULL CITY PRESS
1217 Odyssey Drive
Durham, NC 27713

www.BullCityPress.com

Table of Contents

Acknowledgements:

"He Who Finds It Lives Forever" originally appeared in *Necessary Fiction* (2010)

"Hands to Caskets" originally appeared in *TripleQuick Fiction* (2010)

"If I Had Walked the Moon" originally appeared in *Unsaid* (2010)

"A Personal History of Arson" originally appeared in *Puerto del Sol* (2016)

"If the Hum of Bees Flooded Our Ears" originally appeared in *Midwestern Gothic* (2011)

"May This Strap Restrain You" originally appeared in *Necessary Fiction* (2009)

"The Water Cycle" originally appeared in *Emprise Review* (2009)

"Breathe Deep, Duckling" originally appeared in *Phoenix in the Jacuzzi* (2012)

"A Field Guide to Female Anatomy" originally appeared in *Ninth Letter* (2013)

"The Archivist" originally appeared in *Camera Obscura* (2012)

"The Gravity Well" originally appeared in *Drunken Boat* (2012)

An Elegy for Mathematics was originally published by Origami Zoo Press.

10 Permutations on Desire

1. I am here: *I*. I am here and you are there. I am not interested in what lies between us. I am not interested in tin cans and twine. I am not interested in what tethers I have thrown across this continent to see if I can feel you still, a faint tug on the other side.

2. The blue whale migrates from the Arctic to the tropics, over 13,000 miles each year. In transit, from cold waters to the dream of a warmer sea, the whale eats nothing for four months. The whale lives upon its stored weight. The whale passes through quiet waters propelled by nothing but its own hunger, a resounding echo that billows back when the song of other whales has faded.

3. I learned your name. I held it beneath my tongue. I rolled it around until it felt foreign, until I couldn't remember what my tongue was for.

4. The mantis shrimp dreams in color, a spectrum sixteen times the strength of human vision. Submerged in water, in shallows that haze the sun, the shrimp's sight still expands beyond the limits of land: every shade the human eye ignores, every hue lapsed to blindness.

5. I learned my voice. I can whisper. I can scream into the crevice of canyons. I can scream and I can scream until my hands shake and my voice falls hoarse, but what good is a scream when it only bounces back? When what I hear is less than tin cans, no twine, only the afterimage of echoing.

6. In dreams, finches replay the melody of their songs. What hums through them ghosts back, a ceaseless signature of time, a song braided to the birdbeat of their small hearts long after the song has passed.

7. A girl can dream. A girl can dream of hands pressed firm against her face, against her wrists and her thighs, against her breastbone and her hips. A girl can dream until she wakes. A girl can wake to nothing but night sweats, sheets soaked with the passing of ghosts.

8. Owls mate for life. They are a pair; they are entwined. If one dies the other closes its eyes, refuses to eat, sits quietly upon a tree branch. The other kills itself with love, a sickness of longing. This is something you should know.

9. There is something else that you should know: that I am as fallible as the earth. That there is a hot-flashed core inside this shell that can break, that will pour open, if you would turn my way just once.

10. There is something I should know, too: what I am learning a shell protects. What a voice can scream across a continent and what a body thrums instead: *I want, I want.* A birdsong beating back, the pulse of your animal heart: a want I spoke but never named, here, *here,* a flood dammed to break.

He Who Finds It Lives Forever

Beyond us, beyond the walled fortress of our city, a woods so thick and deep, we learned as children even our voices would never follow us back. The canopy stretched, farther than vision, an endless plain of greened tufts like a tinted mirror, reflecting the clouds, dense, back on themselves. Above the trees, hawks. Their scanning cries a death knell, carried on wind over city walls, low hymn for food they'd never find, every shrew and rabbit and mouse eaten, every small, shuddering heart devoured.

We knew as children that to go there was to be taken. By the red dog, great and hulking, larger than any canine, a phantom through trees. Our fathers told us he consumed every creature in the forest, laid in wait for travelers, hid beneath bog and brush, crimson fur matching all lack of light. I imagined him those nights awake, huddled beside my brother, thinking only of fangs, white glisten, the last known light. My father told us, as every other father did, that in the absence of hunting, the red dog held a bead of gold beneath his tongue. *He who finds it lives forever*, my father said. Then he laughed, a rough sound, said every man who ever tried never returned, not even his voice.

I rolled the bead inside my brain, as a dog would beneath his tongue. It occupied every empty space between broken stretches of sleep, on walks past the palace, inside the damp cellar where I learned to build the city's canals. Gold, a small gem, malleable enough to pound translucent. I'd seen a priestess hold gold leaf to the sun, gossamer-fine, rare beauty I imagined spun into the shape of a pea, hidden lattice of honeyed light, clamped firm beneath muscle and fang. A bead like a seed, small casing to hold the world. More valuable than breath, if we lived forever, more elemental than the water made to flow through the aqueducts I shaped.

I knew my father was dying when he coughed red into his hand. A scarlet splash, dark and red as the fur I'd dreamed each night, a stain he wiped into his palm before my brother or I could see. I lay awake, listened to my brother breathe beside me, envied the quiet of the air through his mouth, the lack of razored teeth through his sleep. The pulse of his lungs, easy match for the ways a tongue can move, rhythmic, across the smooth-worn surface of gold.

An idea came to me, the morning I found a bin of bloodied rags behind our home, discarded. The same morning in the cellar when my master said our water would dry out, when he stood before a map of the city, ran his calloused fingers across the grid of palace and village, let them trail off past the fortressed walls. I watched his fingers move. I knew the contours of the land, that the forest sat above us. Our city, its basin. That to drink, to bathe, to live the way we knew would call upon gravity, continuous flow, the pull of the earth from the forest's dark peak.

I found my father sitting on a stool, behind our home when I came back, the bin of rags gone though one snaked from his pocket, unbloodied, a muted net to catch his cough. Father, I said, and he looked up at me, and we both knew.

There is an aquifer, I said. He turned away from me. He knew where.

I am young, I said. I am expendable.

What I wanted to tell him was that I would find it. I would make him live forever.

But *you are an idiot* is all he said, and he pulled his rag from his pocket and coughed, a smattering of cherried dots. I watched the bright red and thought of fur, crimson coat, felt the fear drain from my skin. How I would go regardless, how I would pry open the dog's mouth. How I would pull the bead from his muscled tongue. A tongue strong enough to lick fur clean from shrews, to conceal the sheen of gold, but no match for my father's, sharp enough to lash, to kill my voice before the woods unearthed the sound to keep.

Hands to Caskets

On the day of my grandmother's funeral, you drove us across the grid of the city, station to station, to find gas below three dollars. A game, when nothing else was—not the way my grandmother collapsed, not the emergency calls while we were out eating lunch, and not the hurricane that blew inland over Louisiana, just days before, destroying every oil platform and refinery in the Gulf of Mexico, alongside everything else.

You were a pallbearer, palms to casket, your fingers staining imprints, ghosts against wood. In the car, after the service and before the burial, I looked out the window while you drove us everywhere, gas light on low. You smiled at every awning, every sign, *not that one,* and *still too high*, until we finally found one station, the cheapest, some sanctuary, game over.

At the cemetery, I held your hand that had held her, from the chapel to the car and from the car to lower her down to some gentler hand of earth. As the pastor spoke you whispered against my ear, *we're only pretending everything ends,* and I blinked across the grass toward a field beyond our gathering. I watched a wren land on a tree branch so I wouldn't watch her go. I pulled my hand from yours and closed my eyes, but your shape stayed there next to me, hovering ghost, some presence in the wake of every absence.

Sometimes, all we can do is stand next to one another.

In the car on the way home, you wondered aloud if gas prices would recede and I watched the streetlights flash past and mouthed a small prayer, some gratitude for you. For hands to carry us, for games to pretend, for the forethought to see beyond a car moving across highway, beyond flood and deluge toward a tide that rolls away, leaving barren beach, pockmarked shore, a place washed clean but for the hollows of scars.

If I Had Walked the Moon

I'd have planted down stakes.

Not rods, not poles, to hold a flag that failed us—for what's a nation, now? You never knew the word.

I'd have dug my stakes deep, into mineral, into basalt. Into solid terrain that fooled us, uninhabitable, and sent us home to a world that blinked bright, hurtled us open-eyed into the future, white hot. We blazed, arms race to space race, mottled meteor shuttling light until our heat, whipped by wind, burned low and quivered out.

Once, we moved against the sun. Once, we had waxen wings.

If I'd known everything then, I'd have pierced my stake into cratered soil. Pockmarked, all the more beautiful in its flaws, visible now from the window above your bed, so close, impossible in proximity. You sigh, you roll over. I rub the small space of your back. You breathe air in your sleep, air no longer safe, air filtered through the closed walls of our barren, sheltered house, through pumps strained free of toxin.

There were seasons, once. Maple trees blazed the color of our ash-darkened sky. There were daffodils and lily pads and weeping willows that grazed their soft limbs against the peach-skin of our cheeks. The trees breathed. They held the memory of our weight.

Before you, I was a raider. Before I pushed you from my body, I pushed this country, now only scorched soil, from the borders of our town. We held a line, arm to arm. We pushed rakes, we pushed hoes. We scraped our hands across the earth. I pulled radishes, carrots, beets and turnips from the hard-packed loam. I sliced them, thin to feed so many mouths, to sustain ourselves, the only unit left. But poison leaked, snaking veins through dirt that branched beneath our lines, pumped tainted blood into the roots of our gardens.

Everything died away. We succumbed. And now, you. All that is left.

Once, there was a television. There was a man in grained image, floating peacefully over rock. There was hope, some promise of peace, one that smoothed the skin across my mother's forehead as we watched, peeling softened potatoes.

I wish you'd known such promise. I wish you'd known your grandmother.

If I had walked the moon, I'd have sown new roots. I'd have borne us all away, built a whole new earth upon the learned topography of lunar plains, the new language of other mountains. I'd have planted seeds, not flags. I'd have let the crust tell me how to work through its rocks. I'd have curled you inside a crater, some snail shell of safety, instead of hurtling back to earth to accolades and exploration, where we'd burn every field and choke.

A Personal History of Arson

Picture frames. Photo albums. Family portraits, snapshots, matte prints.

Known melting points: aluminum, 1220 degrees Fahrenheit. Polystyrene: 266 degrees. Copper: 1083 degrees.

Beware assuming gas burners as cause. Even every burner activated full blast leaves no room for combustion due to drafts, due to cracks in windows and between floorboards and among bricks and the gaps of screened windows, keeping gas below the danger of a flash point, all of which leak air from a home, imperceptibly, all of the time.

Dishes. Wedding china. Flatware. Antique silver, ladles, cutting boards, spoons. Steel: 1400. Ethyl alcohol: 1540. Gasoline: 1490. Stove propane: 1778.

Magnets collected from family travels: Nashville. Yellowstone. Bar Harbor, Maine. Sarasota, Myrtle Beach, the Wisconsin Dells, the Grand Canyon.

Calcium, bone: 1547.

Human skin: just 162 degrees between flame and disintegration.

Beware the kitchen. Beware oil. Vegetable, animal, fish, linseed, corn, olive, sunflower: every oil except mineral, the potential to ignite spontaneously.

Boxed cereal, dried pasta, crackers. Canned tomatoes and beans and beets. A spice rack of cinnamon, curry powder, turmeric, paprika. A refrigerator impervious to burning, left standing and full of half-spoiled milk, plain yogurt, hardened cheese, a half-dozen mottled eggs. Wilting lettuce, jars of mayonnaise and mustard and pickles, apples and potatoes and pears still intact, their solid roundness untouched by flame.

Beware open windows, the drafts of which offer false points of origin. Beware wind, the pulling of air, large areas of damage made to look like a source.

Drapes, curtains, window blinds, doorknobs. Light fixtures and light bulbs, a cracking hiss as their glass heats and explodes. Ironing board. So many clothes. Stockings, leggings, wool socks, corduroy pants and jeans and sweatpants, collared shirts and a cacophony of tees gathered from sporting events, thrift stores, marathons, vacations. Knit hats and mittens and gloves, scarves and earmuffs and swimsuits and beach towels.

Beware charcoals. Hickory. Oak. Ash. All impulsively sparked to flame. Coffee tables. Couches. Inherited side tables and buffets, passed down from grandparents and great-grandparents. Bookcases full of children's books, reference books, classics of literature, a single baby book.

Carbon dioxide at six percent: headache, dizziness, drowsiness.

Carbon dioxide at 10 percent: a lack of breathing.

Carbon dioxide: heavier than air. Forms pockets of lethal concentration.

Beware a history: folded notes, movie tickets stubs, bottle caps, blown-out birthday candles, school photos. Diaries with tiny keys, journals of drawings, sketches of teachers and peers and turning maples beyond the classroom window. A miniature box of porcelain kittens, tiny owls, small frogs, a miniscule gumball machine. A jewelry box: emerald earrings. Collected necklaces. Textbooks wrapped in brown grocery bags. A bag of gemstones.

Fool's gold. Glow-in-the-dark stars stuck to a charred ceiling.

Beware investigation: mine for mental state. Determine cause and origin. Secure medical records. Obtain fire reports from chief officers, establish condition of found building. Inspect for bruises, broken bones. Make maps, diagrams, sketches. Note a pugilistic position. Note a charring of skin, or else not: split skin. Bone fractures emanating outward. Loss of tissue. Steam blisters. Soot in mouth, nostrils. Indication of carbon dioxide in the bloodstream, lividity in colored patches as blood settles. Note particular damage to the head, indication of malicious intent. Note visible bite marks, claw marks, stab wounds, bullet wounds, defense wounds, cuts.

Wrap in cloth sheets. Preserve the clothing.

Remove dentures, bridgework, false teeth. Canvass for witnesses.

Surround what remains. Take photographs.

Preserve all artifacts, everything saved.

Beware shattered porcelain. Coffee mugs. Broken pieces of Mickey Mouse's ears brought home from Disney World driving through the night from Florida to the Midwest, the highway's center line a mirrored flash to the sky's stars. Plastic flatware. Melted in cupboards. Cups and wine glasses without stems and burst bottles of Pinot Noir. Puffed coats. Missouri winter. A black leather jacket stuffed in the back on closet. Love letters. Notes saved from junior high, from anniversaries, birthdays, Valentine's Day. Bubbled handwriting dotted with hearts. The salt taste of sweat. Threads of hair still-clinging to a mattress, afternoon light slanting through windows and kaleidoscoping the walls.

Baby book of inked footprints, smudged palm prints. Small as ducklings, thimbles. Beginnings. *The Cat in the Hat. Goodnight Moon.* This book belongs to. Soccer ball. Jersey knit shorts and dry-fit shirts and the spikes of cleats clotted with grass. Mix tape. Videotape. Board games. Monopoly. Candyland. Hungry Hungry Hippos. Monkeys in a Barrel. Lincoln Logs. Tarot cards and playing cards and a Ouija board used only once, a sixth-grade sleepover when the planchette moved and so many hands flinched away.

If the Hum of Bees Flooded Our Ears

Tom picked up bees by their wings as a child. He sought their striped, downy shapes beneath blades of grass, inside logs of rotted wood. He said he hovered over them, once he'd found one, until the bee alighted on the head of a dandelion or crawled buzzing from knots of lumber. Once it was still, he pinched his thumb and forefinger around one wing and held his breath.

He told me this the night his father left them, after he'd come home from bussing tables and found his mother sitting on the front steps alone, crying, wiping her shirtsleeves against her face when he walked up.

I asked him what he held his breath for, since he was taking the risk anyway, picking up bees. We were sitting on my back porch, away from my parents inside watching *Wheel of Fortune*, and the show's piped-in applause warbled through the open screens of our house, curling into the smoke Tom exhaled from his cigarette.

He squinted out into the night. I think I waited every time, he said, for one of those bees to sting me. They never did. Though once, one bit me.

I laughed. Bees don't bite, I said. The television cut to commercial break inside.

He looked at me. This one did, he said. Something in his voice made me feel bad for laughing, like we weren't talking about bees.

Anyway, it doesn't matter, he said. My dad's never coming back.

I didn't know what to tell him so I asked instead, why bees, why ever pick them up at all.

Tom was quiet for awhile, staring again out into the yard, at the play set my brother and I shared as kids, the chains and poles rusted over, red-brown. He crushed the light of his cigarette beneath his sneaker and when he turned his head my way, his face looked ten years older than it was.

Maybe I knew it then, he said. All that risk wrapped up in a single wing, and pulling it close like that, I don't know. He looked away.

I felt my heartbeat flood my ears, he whispered.

I thought then of when I'd first met Tom, in biology freshman year, and how I'd known who he was before, the only person at our high school who wore headphones everywhere, but we hadn't been friends until we dissected a baby shark together, identifying its rubbery innards, scrubbing the fish oil from our hands in the bathroom sink afterward. I'd asked him about the headphones once, why he didn't just wear ear buds, some small headset, like everyone else. He looked at me like that was a dumb question. He said his headphones felt like an anechoic chamber, and I'd nodded like I knew, then went home and looked the words up in the dictionary my parents kept downstairs.

Tom stopped talking, just stared out across the backyard, and I remembered something my dad told me once, after my own parents had fought and my mother took off for what ended up being only an afternoon, when I'd come downstairs to find him looking out the window toward the driveway where her tires had screeched their departure. He turned my way, looked back out the window. He said sometimes people don't want advice. Sometimes they just want you to sit there and listen to them. So I sat next to Tom quiet, and let him smoke two more cigarettes through the final round of the game show floating through the house and out into the night. Inside all that hush I heard only bees, suspended there buzzing so close to Tom's skin, paper wings dissolving beneath the acid of his fingertips, their hum loud enough to swallow the world.

A Hummingbird Comes to the Feeder

SUNDAY, 4:58 P.M.

A hummingbird comes to the feeder. A feeder I placed beyond my window, its red platform an invitation. A hummingbird comes and I go to the window. The hummingbird flies away.

MONDAY, 8:47 A.M.

A hummingbird comes to the feeder. Its soft drone skirts the edge of the platform. The bird alights and its needle-nose finds the nectar, sugar water I've boiled. It is bigger than hummingbirds from home, a landscape six states away. I try to take its picture from behind the blinds, hidden from view. I try to prove that both of us are here.

TUESDAY, 8:32 P.M.

A hummingbird comes to the feeder. A flash of green against the marbled sun. I watch from behind the blinds and imagine its heartbeat, a mathematics. I imagine I can hear the pulse of a thousand beats in the lone space of a minute, the minute it takes to call home from here, a place of lower elevation, a flatter landscape. The hummingbird moves before a minute can pass.

WEDNESDAY, 11:23 A.M.

A hummingbird comes to the feeder. It perches and stays, more than a minute, more than the interval of its unknowable heartbeats. I watch from inside the window, the logic of our separate hearts. One thousand beats per minute to sixty. Sixty beats per minute to eighty, a new elevation. Eighty beats and still, nothing to one thousand.

There is a syllogism of the heart, here.

There is a syllogism I cannot map.

THURSDAY, 6:49 P.M.

A hummingbird comes to the feeder. It comes while I make dinner, as if we are tablemates. As if I haven't pushed myself over this landscape alone. As if I haven't brought a feeder across two thousand miles of highway for this reason, some companion to ease this ache. The hummingbird lands, then flies away.

The nectar I made is receding.

FRIDAY, 10:01 A.M.

The hummingbird comes to the feeder. It is the same one, I know. It has staked its claim, a territory among territories, its wings alighting on the edge of a country. One that belongs to the bird and to me, a country from another country, what terrain I brought from the plains of the Midwest. A country where only ants overtook the feeder's red lip, drawn to sugar heat on the steam of summer air, a humidity that finds no place here where sun cracks the land.

There is no water. There is only heat.

A dry heat and a lone hummingbird, its heartbeat a mathematics I cannot read.

SATURDAY, 9:58 A.M.

The hummingbird comes to the feeder. I have forgotten to refill it. The hummingbird pokes and cocks its head, then quickly flies away.

I want to say I am sorry.

I want to say I am sorry, in a language we both know.

SUNDAY, 8:28 P.M.

The hummingbird comes to the feeder. I have boiled water and sugar. The nectar will dwindle and I will boil again, then again and again and again. The hummingbird comes to the feeder and the blinds are open. The bird's wings still to a shudder and it drinks the nectar and I imagine its heart slowing its pace, a match for mine.

I am elevated. My eighty beats are stilled.

I am elevated and there is no camera.

There are six states. There is no camera to capture us.

May This Strap Restrain You

It started so easily, a single October second, the movement of tendons and bones that felt habitual within Thomas's hands, not theft but an action without judgment, nothing more than the transfer of metal and leather from one dark place to another. It was something others could have done at no expense, the kind of thing Thomas had seen done a thousand times without the stitches of regret he now felt. Like when Charlotte had scratched a mosquito bite and scarred herself, but told their mother she'd been cut by bullies with pocketknives. Or the time Dahlia had eaten the last of Charlotte's Halloween candy, knowing full well that Charlotte had been saving her cherry Pez packets at the very bottom of her trick-or-treat bag.

This had started with a taunt—this had started with pride. *Come on, Thomas. Or are you scared?* They had chided him, goading him as they always had into following them when they knew he couldn't, but he was older now, old enough to go. *We won't tell mom and dad, but you might. Come on, Thomas, be brave now. Don't be a tattletale like you always are.*

And so he had followed them, Dahlia and Charlotte, out the window and down the smooth bare tree limbs, onto their bikes and he on Charlotte's rear-tire pegs, the chill of motion blowing the autumn night under his jacket and down his spine. Charlotte pedaled faster, keeping time with Dahlia's whirring spokes, and soon there it was, Sycamore Lane, the signpost staining a misgiving into his heart that deepened once they had pedaled further and he saw the dilapidated structure itself.

The Sycamore Hills Asylum—its remnants still stood although the operation had long since been abandoned, once lobotomies were outmoded and even electroconvulsive therapy had become a treatment of the past. The *shocker* remedy, Thomas heard Charlotte and Dahlia call it, as they whispered in their room after their parents had gone to bed, his ear to the door, breath held to a standstill. He knew they had seen the tables, the wristbands, the shackles left behind, on the occasions that they'd snuck out of the house and into the abandoned building. His interest in tagging along had always burned as a smarting curiosity, but now, now that he'd grown a little, and now that he was standing in front of the structure—its façade even more imposing in the full moonlight—he no longer understood why he had wanted to come.

Looking back, he knew he'd taken it just to get it over with—to prove to his sisters that he too was fearless, and to hasten away from the asylum in the wind-burned night, for the safety of his quilted bed. They had gone inside. They had seen the tables. He had stood motionless, staring at their decaying fabrics and rusted metals, until his eyes settled on a restraining strap, hanging slack from the edge of one corroded table. His breath caught then, suspended as if upon a fulcrum inside the walls of his small, shuddering chest, and then he'd seized the strap, its leather pulling easily away from the table, and stuffed it into his coat pocket. His sisters had watched him with gleaming eyes, Dahlia nodding her approval, and then they'd hurried from the building and jumped back on their bikes, the night trailing their wheels like phantoms.

He had kept it, crammed between the mattress and the box spring, its metal buckles, he was sure, grating away the lining of his mattress pad. He felt each part through the thick foam of his bed—

the half-rotten leather, the corrugated clasps, the roughened edges meant to grip the cot-like table. Each piece of hardware, every stitch through the strap's worn fabric filled the corners of the bedroom, but Thomas refused to touch the strap again, to let his fingers crawl down the bed lining toward the stolen strip just inches beneath his pillow. He understood now the consequence it had brought.

• • •

It only took a week for Thomas to first feel the effect of what he'd done, during the second nuclear detonation drill that his school administered. Duck and cover exercises, Crittendon Elementary was calling them, and he didn't quite understand the purpose—hiding under a desk with heads covered wouldn't save them, nothing would, but he followed orders anyway, not wanting his name on the blackboard. An alarm bell sounded the drill and Thomas scrambled beneath a table bearing microscopes and preserved amphibians, all of which would be destroyed as well if a nuclear cloud ever bloomed above their school. Thomas expected to be alone, but once he pushed past the tablecloth, a faint gasp escaped his mouth when he found Arthur Dayton there as well, crouched low and picking the rubber sole from his shoe, a boy he'd never talked to but who had always seemed friendly.

What's your name? Arthur asked, even though there were only forty children in their entire class, but Thomas disguised his hurt by replying in kind.

Arthur was funny, making jokes about the duck and cover drills that made Thomas giggle out loud before covering his mouth in shame, hoping he would not get in trouble. Arthur said his family had a bomb shelter in their cellar, stocked with a two-year supply of water and dehydrated food, and flares and candles and extra clothing for every type of weather. They had sweaters, snow boots, extra Hanes t-shirts, mittens. Arthur invited Thomas to come over to see it sometime, the shelter was full of all kinds of neat things, and they could walk down to the trading card shop afterward if Thomas liked baseball cards. Thomas said his favorite player was Hank Aaron, and Arthur agreed. Thomas's chest wavered then, just as it had when he pulled the strap from Sycamore Hills—upon Arthur's voice, its upward lilt of agreement, and the way his eyes burned still-green through the table's cloaking shadow.

And it was that palpitation, a cadenced trembling, that Thomas felt grow into a rapid-fire symphony within his ribcage when he was falling asleep that night, his eyes wide open, his head muddled and swimming, the strap resting immobile under the mattress beneath him. His breath caught in his chest, the same choked humming he'd felt in the asylum and there beneath the table, faltering inside Arthur's watchful glance, and the weight of that likeness bore down upon his ribs then, stealing his breath almost entirely. The strap lay inert, static inside cloth and fabric, and Thomas let his fingers creep steadily down the mattress, to make contact, to apologize. But his chest moved, a thudding metronome, and Thomas pulled his hand away, tucked it securely beneath his pillow as the vibrations invaded his body, ran the length of his extremities and into the inner recesses of his brain, a sensation that might have been inexplicable had it not so clearly begun with Arthur.

• • •

Thomas felt himself changing, and he could not undo it. And this, he now knew, was the consequence. It was the burden that followed him, the reparation he would make, the outcome of so many sins—pride and greed, and now lust—that would pursue him for retribution. He wished now, with every fiber of his small being, that he could put the strap back. That he could remove the leather belt from beneath his mattress, that he could maneuver the bicycle spokes backward in time, that he could return the metal buckles to their rightful place.

But he could not, he knew. Even if he climbed out alone, withstood the midnight air whistling past his ears in banshee screams, even if he restored the strap, better suited now for ghosts, the damage was irrevocably done.

Dahlia mentioned it only once, their mother in the kitchen washing dishes, and Charlotte smirking there beside her sister, a wordless taunt across the table. *Whatever happened to your strap,*

Thomas? Did you tie up some poor kitten or squirrel? And he'd looked away, slid from his seat, had taken his plate into the kitchen to be cleaned.

Arthur asked him at school, while he sat on the playground's swing set alone, would he still come over to see the shelter, just as they had talked about? But Thomas only shook his head, feigned ignorance and walked away across the playground, pretended Arthur had imagined the conversation, that they'd never spoken. And in his desk chair that afternoon, his eyes on his notebook while Arthur sustained furtive glances across the aisle, Thomas refused to look up, declined to acknowledge what he knew was in the periphery, impossible. He would live with this, until the strap disintegrated in its own decay, until there never was a drill in which Arthur had made him laugh.

How to Let Go

Imagine yourself in a bubble.

A vacuum. A choked cylinder. A space capsule.

Imagine yourself untethered, without wire, without strand or filament, without every bond that will break you inevitably and entirely.

Imagine yourself as a cloud, unbounded. Imagine your weight as inconsequential as the element of air, that for once you hold no stones, that the bricks strapped to your back are a burden you never carried.

Imagine your life, the future—a stretching plain still nebulous but bright, a place that holds no counting and no repeating, no looming stratus you must kill by ritual.

Your rituals are what keep you, soothing balms that cast everything in calm light. They render you liberated, if for only a moment, from the fixed bindings of how this world will end. The end is inevitable, an ending you were born knowing, an ending that wakes you gasping in the middle of the night wondering how everyone else can live with this while you choke on your own breath and swallow gulps of fresh air that you know will one day cease.

You cannot adapt. You watch people in malls, on street corners. You watch the contours of their faces and wonder how they maintain an air of peace, how they can order coffees and smile at salespeople and go about their days, every day, knowing every person on this earth will die.

You count your steps. You back up and retread the same concrete when one stride doesn't feel right, when you step on a crack fissuring the pavement or a discolored patch of gravel. Four steps are good. Six steps, bad. Seven steps are magical. Thirteen steps, the end of everything.

Imagine yourself buoyant, emancipated from rules. Imagine yourself splayed sloppily across the asphalt, your soles bearing down hard upon every fault line and crack.

Imagine that counting your steps can't keep anyone alive.

Imagine not checking each lock, each burner. Imagine not washing your hands, over and over, satisfied at last that soap can cleanse death. Imagine your actions as true and not placation, not sealant keeping the waves of a roiling sea contained.

Imagine a loophole, some tunnel out of your double-bind—that the miraculous thinking of soap and steps is the same force you hold out hope as the motor beneath this world, a mystery and a magic, an unexplained engine that keeps death as only a mask and not the end it is understood to be.

Imagine you grew up with religion. Imagine a certainty of peace beyond ritual. Imagine letting go your grip on each moment, on every birthday and holiday and carved pumpkin and lit tree, every moment you're all there in the fleeting space of the same room.

Imagine you love no one, and no one loves you. Imagine yourself weightless for once, to live without links, to be as unattached as air. Imagine never understanding the complications of falling in love, with your lover's laugh or a chickadee's small wings or the weight of your mother's palm laid gently across the bones of your hands.

Imagine you can hear your heart breaking.

Conserve the sound.

Imagine it's your own death you fear. Imagine circling in.

Imagine that there is purpose in this, in all of this—that there is meaning beyond ritual. Imagine that the world ends in light, that what love floods your veins is a gleaming of stars. Imagine your wires, your filaments, your strings and your bonds. Imagine them as an energy, transmutable, a light bound to your heart in blood.

The Water Cycle

Letterman had gotten through six of his Top Ten when I heard your voice. You were quiet, almost inaudible, and I wondered how long you had been standing there. Not that it mattered, or that I'd been watching anything questionable. But sometimes it made me feel strange, for reasons I can't explain, to think that maybe you knew we had separate lives in some way, and that sometimes we did things that weren't always the same.

You said you couldn't sleep, and you stood there at the bottom of the stairs, your fingers tugging absently at your pajama pants. All the lights in the house were out, and I could barely see you in the television's glow. You wanted a bedtime story, you said. Some girls at school had told you about Bloody Mary today, and though you weren't afraid, you just couldn't sleep was all. You didn't even have a mirror in your room.

I muted the television. In the weak blue light we found the stairs, and you held the banister the entire way up, taking each step with both feet.

After you'd jumped onto your bed and buried yourself in the covers, I sat alongside and asked what you wanted to hear. Your face looked like a moon, the covers pulled to your chin.

Tell me how I began, you said.

But you already know, I said.

You'd heard me say it, what felt like hundreds of times before.

But you were lying, you said, and when you said it, something in my chest twitched, the way horse skin does to shake a fly.

I wouldn't lie, I said, and in some sense, I knew that was true.

Gemma said storks bring babies, you said, eyebrows wrinkled. Her mom told her they bring babies to the hospital, you said, and that you go and pick them up.

I closed my eyes. What I'd told you could stand, at least for tonight.

Gemma didn't tell you that all babies are different, I said. Maybe a bird brought her here, but you came another way.

But how? You looked at me. How did I fall from the sky?

When I looked at you then, I knew that something had come to an end, and that even the greatest of stories wouldn't halt the inevitability of the one I owed you at some future time, in some future room I hoped was not this one.

You fell from the sky, I said.

And there is where I began.

I told you that weather was fickle, that much in the same way hurricanes and thunderstorms and tornadoes pop up in the most unexpected of ways, so too can babies if you're not watching. But I told you I was watching, that I'd been watching and waiting for you, with my eye on one small cloud that had been hovering over my backyard for days. Most clouds move, and they drift along with the winds, but this little cloud stuck around while I watered my herb garden on the back porch, while I read in the afternoons outside. And one day, when it was terribly, terribly hot, I told you I could see the water from a lake nearby gravitating toward the sky, the way it does just before it rains. With that water floating upward— barely visible, but I could see it nonetheless—that little cloud started getting heavier and heavier, and darker and darker. The day got so hot that I almost thought I'd melt, when suddenly that small cloud burst into a million raindrops, and one of them landed in my yard.

I told you I knelt down in the grass where the droplet had landed, and when I did, I saw there was a baby floating inside. But when I tried to touch the raindrop, it popped like a magic bubble. And that's when you tumbled into my arms.

This is what I told you, right through to the end. But by the time I'd told you how it was that you began, you were already asleep, your cheeks puffed and soft. As I headed back down the stairs, toward the light of the muted television, I wondered if now might be the start of something hard, of an inevitable slide toward one terrible moment when I would have to tell you that I was your mother—always, your mother—but not in any manner of blood.

Breathe Deep, Duckling

Keiran says you're not meant for this world. He tells you snails are just snails, when you step on one in the park and feel its shell pop and leak beneath your shoe. He says snails don't deserve tears, nor do fledglings fallen from nests, or veterans without homes, or the elderly couple that walks past your apartment every morning, holding hands, weakening your grasp on soaped dishes as you watch from the kitchen window. This is life, he says. It is what it is. He tells you toughen up, steel yourself against the planet beyond your door or be forever disappointed—that the world's edges aren't as delicate as you imagined, that life moves on and leaves everyone behind. Tough love, he tells you when you make up after fights, a phrase he says you never learned. But he is a beautiful man, his spilled laughter makes you forget every callus, and his hands are just soft enough that sometimes, when he touches you, they feel like the feathered weight of your mother's palms, holding you up, tender beneath your belly as you kicked across the water and learned to swim.

Hold your breath, she'd tell you, before she pushed your head gently under, hand guiding your forehead. She held you for only seconds, suspended beneath the water of the pool in your backyard, increasing by time until you learned to bind your lungs. But underwater felt like death, silent billow of blue, a lack of sound without her that sheathed you in some foreign womb. Every time you surfaced, the air you gasped in washed a monsoon through your body, the sunlight honeyed a warm coat across your hair, and the strands lost their weight through the gentle pull of your mother's hands, so welcome you exploded into giggles. Your mother tickled you, fingers troubling the water beneath your body, and as she laughed you felt her hands hold you only tighter. Duckling, she called you, as adept by sea as you were on land.

Keiran has never known the nickname, a word you've never told him like every other secret you keep. That you capture spiders in paper cups, release them to the porch. That you sing in the car when you are driving alone, that sometimes the weight of your own voice brings you quietly to tears. And that sometimes you laugh so loud in movie theaters that people turn to look at you, something he's never noticed, until he finally suggests a comedy one Saturday and you laugh so hard your voice booms above the surround sound. You don't look at Keiran but you feel him staring at you anyway, the side of your face growing hot. In the car on the way home, he tells you everyone heard, everyone was looking, and his words remind you of sixth grade, the first time the sound felt like something it shouldn't be, when at recess you laughed so loud jumping rope while everyone else just giggled, a crystalline sound, a chandelier. You felt yourself expand beyond your own borders then, as if you lived outside of your body, looking in. You came home and strapped on your swimsuit and crawled into the pool, floating face up, hair billowing out in tentacles, arms extended like a starfish, ears held beneath a silent surface.

When Keiran suggests a walk around the neighborhood, like the old couple he's seen you watching out the windows, you notice the trees bunched with the budding speckles of fruit blossoms, their fragrance through your hair like jasmine. The tips of each tree are so green, so lush, that you can't even remember early spring, slow opening of leaves, the way tree tips unfurl their gentle, grass-stained hands. Keiran says there was nothing you missed, that this happens every year. He tells you seasons are predictable, that what is verdant will soon fade, that rusted brown becomes bare, becomes ice, becomes birth. You consider this, the truth of this world, and as he takes your hand and leads you down the sidewalk, his palm is not your mother's. But you take a breath, inhale the scent of hyacinth, you pull in all the air your lungs will need to sustain your body beneath a soundless surface, to hold your heart underwater.

A Field Guide to Female Anatomy

I. HEAD (CEPHALIC)

MOUTH (ORAL)

FIELD MARKS: Pink in color. Cracked skin. Tongue mottled beneath a wall of teeth. Molar, premolar, incisor, canine. The sharpest hide just beyond the lip.

DESCRIPTION: Trembles when angry or flooded with sorrow. Any combination, all combinations in between. Small enough to go unnoticed. Small enough to obscure the voice. The larynx is what is known, and not the sound it does or does not produce.

EYE (OPTIC)

FIELD MARKS: Two, non-vital. Retina, cornea. Rods and cones. An iris that can be blue, brown, gray, sometimes green: a firework ringed by a circle of black.

DESCRIPTION: Open. Bright. Centered in the midline of the face. Eye contact is obvious, but easy to avoid.

EAR (AUDITORY)

FIELD MARKS: Two, non-vital. Curved lines orbiting a hole that descends to a snail-shelled cochlea, to an eardrum and to the ossicles, the three smallest bones in the body. The bones: hammer, anvil, stirrup. The smallest and yet the loudest. A drum, a hammer. An anvil in wait.

DESCRIPTION: Can be attached or unattached. Can experience punctures, Meniere's or labyrinthitis, all afflictions that tilt the world beyond balance. Can hear talk and more talk, explanations of the world as it is known. Can keep the body awake until headlights pool across the blinds and an engine dies, until the weight of approaching footsteps splits fissures through the floorboards.

NOSE (OLFACTORY)

FIELD MARKS: Two nasal passages connected to the pharynx, the sinus, the Eustachian tube. Slender in shape, belling to nostrils and a cartilage tip. A bridge divides the eyes. A bridge is vulnerable to breaking.

DESCRIPTION: Can be crooked, hooked, blunt or flat. Can be compensated for, can be changed. Can detect scent, most heavily tied to memory. Can detect a child's first birthday in the odor of her clothes, can smell laughter and cake and the helium plastic of balloons. Can detect accumulated sorrow in the salted pores of human skin. Can detect a history of violence in the passing scent of cologne.

NECK (CERVIC)

FIELD MARKS: Slender column that connects the head to the thorax. Contains seven vertebrae. Contains the larynx, invisible to the eye.

DESCRIPTION: Can turn 90 degrees in either direction. Can work in tandem with ears and eyes to keep the body alert. Bears the mark of hickeys. Bears the mark of thumbprints. But more often bears the mark of nothing, the most visible and obvious place.

HAIR (CAPILLUS)

FIELD MARKS: Grows from follicles in brown, yellow, red, black. Can be cut, can be dyed. Can be coarse, fine, thick, curly. Can be lost, through shedding or tearing.

DESCRIPTION: A mark of femininity. A mark of shame. A beacon on street corners when trucks pass, when men lean from windows. A wavering target that what you are is what never belonged, that you are within this world, that you are buried within its core.

II. TORSO (THORAX)

SOLAR PLEXUS (CELIAC)

FIELD MARKS: Abdominal region, sternum to diaphragm; a system of nerves radiating from the core. Where the wind is knocked. Where the diaphragm spasms. Where breathing grows difficult when the viscera are blown.

DESCRIPTION: A valley, a cave. One that can be pushed against a wall or the threading of a bed. What matters is that the plane can take it. What matters is that the plane is not the neck.

BREAST (MAMMARY)

FIELD MARKS: Two, non-vital. Peaks of flesh on the anterior of the torso, potentially varying in size. Situated opposite the shoulder blades, upon the breastbone. A bone that, if the skin is stretched, reveals what holds the heart.

DESCRIPTION: You were without them, once. You were without them until they grew. You were without them until they imposed themselves upon you, until boys snapped your training bra, until you learned to live with this weight and not because you wanted to.

SHOULDER BLADE (SCAPULA)

FIELD MARKS: Two ridges twinning the posterior of the torso, mimicking the shape of folded bird wings.

DESCRIPTION: The wings are folded. They are waiting beneath skin. What matters is not that they are folded. What matters is that they can unfold.

COLLARBONE (CLAVICLE)

FIELD MARKS: Thin ridge along the shoulders. Clearly visible, a bulge in the skin.

DESCRIPTION: Considered beautiful in its curvature. A magnet for palms, fingerprints, mouths. A vessel of memory for what it once meant to be held, a ghost of shared breath in the arc of the bone.

PELVIS (SACRUM)

FIELD MARKS: Holds the uterus, the ovaries. The urethra, the rectum, the vagina. A frame embracing what worlds will come.

DESCRIPTION: Remember this – how hands felt as they unfastened your jeans. How there was a first time for this, once. How there was a tug, a soft weight, how that weight was unbearable in light. How your body razed itself from the inside, how you burned yourself to the ground. How sex is a skill, perfected through years of wanting and razing and salivating and destroying and how even still there is light, the featherweight of hands waiting to unravel you. How they fumble across your belt buckle. How a match ignites.

NAVEL (UMBILICUS)

Field Marks: Circular mark in the center of the abdomen, where the umbilical cord was cut. Varies in size, shape, concavity or protrusion. An indelible shape of separation, of what it means to be divided.

Description: When you are alone, your hands stretch over your separation. When you are alone, your mother finds you in the weightlessness of your hands. Her hands, now your hands, how soft they once were. How there is nothing left upon your stomach but a specter of severance. When you are not alone, a tongue skirts your skin with no gentleness of a mother. A tongue skirts your skin and only teeth will follow.

III. EXTREMITIES (MEMBRUM)

FINGERNAIL (UNGUIS)

Field Marks: Keratin sheath across the dorsal tip of the finger. Both opaque and translucent, moon-shaped and hard. Grows approximately three millimeters in a month, beyond notice. Steady, surely.

Description: Can be filed down, can be painted. Can trap skin cells and caked dirt. Can be bitten to the quick beneath talk. Beneath more talk. Can rake the flesh from skin if threatened or pinned.

KNUCKLE (METACARPOPHALANGE)

Field Marks: Peaked joints where the finger meets the hand. Ridged when the hand lays flat. Most visible when the hand is clenched into the shape of a fist.

Description: He made a fist once and held it to yours. He told you the fist was the size of the heart. You saw his was larger and you disbelieved. That there is substance in size, that there is merit in scale. That a fist is any substitution for the weight of a heart.

ELBOW (OLECRANON)

FIELD MARKS: Jointed bend where the upper arm and forearm meet. Allows the arm to bend 180 degrees. Moves the hand forward and away from the body. Forms a weapon if thrust.

DESCRIPTION: One of the only locations of the body without feeling or nerve. Can be pinched or pulled. Can be prodded without pain. Can hibernate in the winter of a landscape beyond hurt, a deadened island where the body stores the meaning of growing slowly numb.

THIGH (FEMUR)

FIELD MARKS: Upper segment of the leg, thicker in diameter and size. Glides into the kneecap, the shin, the lower extremities of the foot.

DESCRIPTION: Highly sensitive to touch, a heightened zone of nerve. Can tremble beneath fingertips. Can shudder if stroked. Can heat the palms of hands if held together, the warmest location on the body. Can become a greenhouse, a whole world.

TOE (PHALANX)

FIELD MARKS: Extensions at the end of the foot, increasing in size toward the instep. Bear weight. Provide balance in the movement of walking forward.

DESCRIPTION: A diving board. A threshold. An edge your feet grip. You watch the water drip down, curve around the board, escape into the pool. You are at an edge. You know your toes will push you. You know what weightlessness will come.

HEEL (CALCANEUS)

FIELD MARKS: Blunt surface that forms the posterior base of the foot. Absorbs shock. Stabilizes the sole. Designed to bear the brunt of compressive force.

DESCRIPTION: Blackened by tar from the shingles that hold your feet. You climb from your window and expand upon the roof, to watch the smooth plain of the tree line and the moon rising from it. There is a world there. Beyond talk, beyond weight. You are waiting and you are ready, to scrub away what cakes your soles. You are waiting, ready. To move beyond following, beyond followed, to go where nothing will know to follow.

The Archivist

Julie Powell: 587,436,974 breaths, from the first choking, light-filled gasp to the last exhalation, a dimmed sigh in the darkened oncology corridor of Lincoln Memorial. 91,467 kisses, a low number, her husband a man who shunned her affections, though Julie made up for this on the side with their part-time maid, a secret she kept until the moment of her death, alongside 44 others: that she'd cheated on a chemistry test in the eleventh grade, glancing over Eugene Harrold's shoulder, that she hated her mother's famous lemon cookies, that her husband only made her orgasm twice, though she pretended in shrieking climax more times than she'd been able to count (956 on file).

The Archivist works through these numbers, crunches their specificity, their exactitude, every moment of a life. She compiles every file when the light of living begins to dim, when an ambulance races to the hospital, when a week begins and the air is strange, a fatal accident tingeing its edges, or when a neuron simply misfires, a single misstep toward its final decline. The Archivist waits in poised ready, assembles hundreds of files for the dying perched upon their last threshold. She gathers every moment no one remembers, every toothache, every bitten nail, every mundane July afternoon. Though she is never the one to hand them their file, a side she's never seen, it is her handiwork, a smoothened joy she imagines but has never witnessed, the tally of every hour, every memory, a love letter of their lives to carry them away, a hereafter. And though she straddles that line, the border every human crosses, she remains staunchly planted on this side, neither mortal nor immortal, a stasis so long as mortals die, a job to be done, a bridged stagnation that slowly disbands her, now, now that her son is gone.

[are there regrets?]

She felt the call when she first heard voices, as if a calling were something tangible, as if all humans were born to do one thing, a lie she holds close now, a fallacy. Her existence was to protect, to take care, a failure that crowds the lettering of every file, every measured moment. If it were true that this was her chance, her one thing, she knows now that the fact of her continued, impossible existence proves the lie, the failed act, that there is no one anymore to shelter, nothing left to protect.

And yet, the voices come still—gargled and wavering as if through water, the same voices she heard as a girl, the separate double-speak of dying. As a child she pushed her hands against her own ears, held her head beneath a feather pillow at night and still they came, untethered and floating. A call that they themselves never heard, never knew they emitted, a call she has heard her entire life, a million splintered voices. They come when they wish, while she sleeps, washes dishes, these monotonies of her own life that are catalogued like all the others without want or will, a terrible ticking that once soothed her but now rolls away, a dull drone, interrupted only by the dying and not the tug of small hands, once firm against her hemline.

Steven Larimer: 543 rubber bands bound across attorney-at-law documents, 1,267 boxes of Wheaties consumed, 38 eye infections, a childhood of allergies bloomed to adult conjunctivitis. 94 videotapes of sexual acts, all shot without a partners' awareness or consent, 36 routine teeth cleanings, 4 cavities. Suicide attempts: two, and only one of those, unsuccessful.

The work is a learned detachment, a perfected skill. The Archivist hunches at her desk crouched above each file, computes the numbers by closing her eyes. She knows her body only as conduit, as passage for voice and integer. She has known all her life that this is understood, a crucial fact of duty. This prerequisite of work, to work alone, to channel rather than connect is what haunts her, louder than any human voice, its ringing tenor a reminder of transgression and of punishment and of the penalty itself: a weight heavier than the sum of all calculated, human acts.

[are you scared?]

The Archivist used to watch him, from the perched position of her file-scattered desk. She watched him crawl across the floorboards, pick at specks of dust and crumb with his tiny fingers and felt her breath flood the inflated capsules of her lungs, caught and snagged on every wonderful thing he would be. She imagined a life for him, fully separate from her own, a life of fluttered kisses and skipped heartbeats, of skin brushed intentionally against skin and of immeasurable and buoyant joy, beyond any finite sum she could tabulate or tally. She closed her eyes at night, and through voices and numbers wished the future would bear him far away from here, from this run-down apartment, far from every entrapment of her servitude to this world.

Water and light shape all landscapes, The Archivist knows, a fact that despite her entrenched separation from this earth bred a beauty she once revered. The desert: full sun, and so little water, a parched terrain. The rainforest: partial sun, and more water than a landscape can hold. And her own cloistered apartment, separate from the earth, little sun and even less water: only enough to submerge, to drown everything from this world.

Jennifer Tremont: 4,593 cups of tea, all of them green. 3,923 bursts of laughter, 2,458 comic books read, 2 penned herself, only one of them shared, with her mother before she passed away. 590 rainy days endured, 3 broken umbrellas, all discarded in sidewalk trashcans. 389 meals out for Chinese dim-sum, her favorite on Sunday mornings after crosswords, 947 grids completed. Black eyes: nine. One broken collarbone, three bloody noses. Calls to helplines: three. Visits to group therapy: three. Threats to leave: nineteen.

Violent partners: one. The only one needed.

The Archivist has seen more paths to death than she's ever known to name. This calculation, one she has turned away from, a sum only of sorrow: a catalogue of fallibility that disheartens her to chart. She had started out as a girl considering only the most obvious, only old age, only the peaceful descent into sleep that could take a human quietly and not the homicides, the lethal injections, the battered rapes and domestic disputes. They are a sidenote, separate from her indexes, but they are there, nonetheless, a list always equated as one, an ending impossible to evade.

[sometimes I can't breathe, a weight crushing my lungs]

The Archivist's apartment: a wasteland, a coffin. A desk, one chair, a small table, a bed. An efficiency elevated above a bustling, nameless city, a tenement among tenements, a small square in a grid meant to obscure her. And her place in this world, one of balance, an acrobatic walk—to be within this world, to be without it, to stride a line as thin as spiderwebbed silk. The life of a ghost, she could imagine, if not for this ache, acute and unbroken. A reminder, a constant that not even ghosts suffer an in-between like this, their bodies diaphanous, neither skin nor nerve to kill.

Casey Albright: These, the worst. The ones that were always hard, that have now become impossible.

Casey Albright: Zero cigarettes smoked, zero trees climbed, zero books read and relished as favorites, zero love letters hidden beneath mattress and box spring. Twelve toys accumulated, three baby blankets, 468 blinks of his eyes and 45 kisses, all from his parents before he gasped his final breaths, an end The Archivist knew but still squeezed her eyes against as Casey lay in his crib, as he quietly stopped breathing, a death doctors would attribute to SIDS without explanation.

[is my laughter still trapped in the walls?]

The Archivist knows this, too, beyond water and sunlight, beyond desert or oasis—the frailties of all humans, the greatest folly she's learned. The sum total of these tallies, in the end, beyond cans of soup consumed, beyond letters handwritten: a dulled monotony, a glazed blindness of habit. The learned assumption that because a life moves, sunrise, sunset, because nothing ever changed, that this has always meant, of course, that nothing ever would.

Brendan West: 19 Major League Baseball stadiums visited, 216 small-venue shows and arena concerts attended, 587 albums purchased and cradled inside headphones against his ears, 43 mixtapes compiled. 342 sighs on rainy days, 103 smiles at his brother's newborn child, both in person and by mere thought alone, and four true heartbreaks, three by love and one, the one he never mentioned, by the split-seconded tear of ACL, a tear that ripped from root the growing dream of a mid-level soccer career.

The Archivist admits to herself now that it was his body she noticed, the smooth chiseling of a once-runner's calves. A quiet throbbing, her half-human failing, a dull ache that she never knew a piercing hurt could ever replace, a relentless magnet that drew her to his hospital room, a silent harbinger above him, a point of contact she was never meant to breach. He lay in a coma, a final sleep she saw clearly as she tabulated his laughter, his appetites, his breaths and his transgressions—a reckless driving record not among them, a clean past that bore no foretelling of other drivers beyond the grip of his own hands placed firmly upon a steering wheel.

The Archivist considers now, still, what it was about him, what it was that drew her to scale the walls to his hospital bed, to close the doors to his room, to hover above him and straddle him. The straddling, a familiar act: not in practice but in habit, her body a conduit, a natural bridge from life to death. A line she walked by routine every day of her life, a line that always lead, she knows now, to this single, fixed point.

The Archivist recognizes the splitting instant that turns, the flash-burned fulcrum of before, of after, the way a single second can hold the dagger and the flame to rip a gaping wound so wide, to sear a chasm, to raze the known world to scorched, rubbled ash. The before: a car, an accident, a career, a life alone. The after: a dying man, the most beautiful man she'd ever seen, and a transgression, her own, a single lovely mistake, a consequence in spades.

And the boy, the one that split from seed inside of her, as she lay beside the sleeping man all night in his hospital bed before daybreak. As she pretended, only for a stretch of dark hours, that the tabulated sighs and skipped heartbeats of human love were hers for a moment, hers alone: a glitch, a mistake, one that corrected itself in time.

[lift the tile, the one beneath the bathtub faucet. there, you will find my name]

The Archivist's apartment: a bathtub. Untended while the water still filled, if for only a moment. A shrieking call, a file scrawled and prepared. A distraction of voice and integer, a single second, an apartment where small hands could map its narrow contours palm to budding palm but big enough still, to swallow their splashing, to silence a lapping before a mother's hands could reach and pull him from the water. This drowned weight, a mother carries: a punishment heavier than the featherweight of lust, than every silence a room can hold.

[lift the tile, the one beneath the bathtub faucet. my name, written before you sealed it]

The Archivist's child: unarchivable, a voice she still hears. A voice that never came to her, never whistled, never called. A voice that calls only now, fills the apartment, crowds a silence she once considered intolerable.

[my name. my name and yours]

A retiling, once: the only improvement ever made toward a home. His name, hers, sealed and caulked to look back from an older age, a grown life. A dream, her own, a quantified dream as picket fences, as cats and children, the wishes of the dying she's seen so many times, the tallied, sated goals. And the line, one she holds now, a disconnected breach: her sentence only one to fill, beyond duty, a dream that stays with her only in song, in ghosted, separate voice.

Timothy Krakauer, Kara Johnson, Alice Chan, Dorothea Jones.

Beneath the tile, his small handprints, his initials, her name.

Darren Moseley, Althea Roberts, Julius Darringer, Ben Albertson.

Calculated sums, concrete integers. The living still die though The Archivist dreams it now, a world without end. A world without files, without numbers, without light or water or lungs. Yet the voices still come. And through their calls, the one that saturates the room, a ghost she waits to take shape: a blinking hope to become body, to bleed this through, to slice a wound deep enough to break every layer of skin, to tip the fulcrum and to plunge straight through bone. A wound to savor, the only one needed, to bear a world away.

The Gravity Well

Sarah tells me that we are ghosts, all of us. She says that ghosts are nothing more than afterimages of ourselves, or pre-images, that blurred streaks and blown-open doors are only our own bodies in some parallel space, passing through the same rooms we once occupied, rooms we will occupy, rooms we settle into right now.

Sarah began talking like this when her amniotic membrane ruptured.

When I brought her home from the hospital, she lay in bed for two days, lights dimmed. I went to the pharmacy, filled her pain prescription, stood in line too close to the seasonal aisle, the sidewalk chalk and water guns. That night, as I lay next to her watching the ceiling, waiting to fall asleep, she told me through the dark that the earth felt like an anchor, that gravity detained her, a drowned weight.

I thought she meant the pressure. I thought she meant a weight of absence so vast, and not the ways that gravity holds time.

I went to work, organized my pencils. I drank five cups of coffee and waited until mid-morning to call home, and when I did, Sarah never answered, she must have been sleeping. But when I came home from work, she was sitting up in bed reading. She didn't even look up.

Did you know everything is relative? she asked. And then she mentioned ghosts, how so many iterations of ourselves split apart inside the earth's pull.

Sarah says we are elsewhere, always. That there are versions of both of us sliding through other planes, all the time. She says there are loopholes, that the right energy opens their channels, prevents their collapse. She says our baby didn't really die, that she is with us somewhere else, some other space in time. When she says this, I want to believe her. But all I imagine are two panes of glass, sliding past each other with nothing in between.

When Sarah finally got out of bed, we went to the park. We sat on a blanket in the shade and watched people walk their dogs, read on benches. We watched two kids fly a kite in a nearby field. Gravity controls the passage of time, Sarah said to me, though her gaze followed the kids. Because we're here, on this planet, we have no concept of how time can shift.

She told me we are a gravity well, that light blueshifts and contracts in this unbearable core of pressure. She said that light expands as it moves away, a redshift, and though her eyes turned toward the sky, away from the kids and from me, her hands moved to her belly, settled there on what light got away.

I think of this while she sleeps, how light is trapped by gravity, how time is bound by light. I want to believe her but I am sinking, this elsewhere too gleaming to bear. Our ghosts are enough for Sarah. They are not enough for me. I think of gravity, what black holes can swallow, how nothing, not even light, finds a path of escape. I watch the ceiling and listen to Sarah breathe and imagine I am hovering above both of us, watching myself sleep, a ghost untethered in light.

Anne Valente is the author of a short story collection, *By Light We Knew Our Names* (Dzanc Books, 2014), and a novel, *Our Hearts Will Burn Us Down* (William Morrow/HarperCollins, 2016). Her fiction appears in *One Story, The Kenyon Review, The Southern Review* and *Ninth Letter*, and her essays appear in *The Believer* and *The Washington Post*. Originally from St. Louis, she currently teaches creative writing at Hamilton College.